D1106329

In the Hindu tradition,
Ganesha is one of the most worshipped gods. He has the body
of a man and the head of an elephant. Ganesha is the master of
obstacles—mostly their remover, but sometimes their placer.
He also has a sweet tooth, so be sure to always have some lotus
cakes on hand when you walk through the forest.

*It is with honor, affection, and gratitude toward the
Hindu faith that Ganesha inspired this story.*

## To Maeve and Ash:

This book is for you. May you always remember that life is unfolding *for* you, even—and especially—when you think it's not. It might just be Ganesha trying to show you a new way.

Text copyright © 2021 by Margo Buchanan. Illustrations copyright © 2021 by Becky James.

ISBN: 978-1-7371372-0-7

*Published by:*
Margo Buchanan
www.therockcollectorbook.com

*Illustrated by:*
Becky James
www.beckyjamesillustrates.com

FIRST EDITION
Printed in Canada

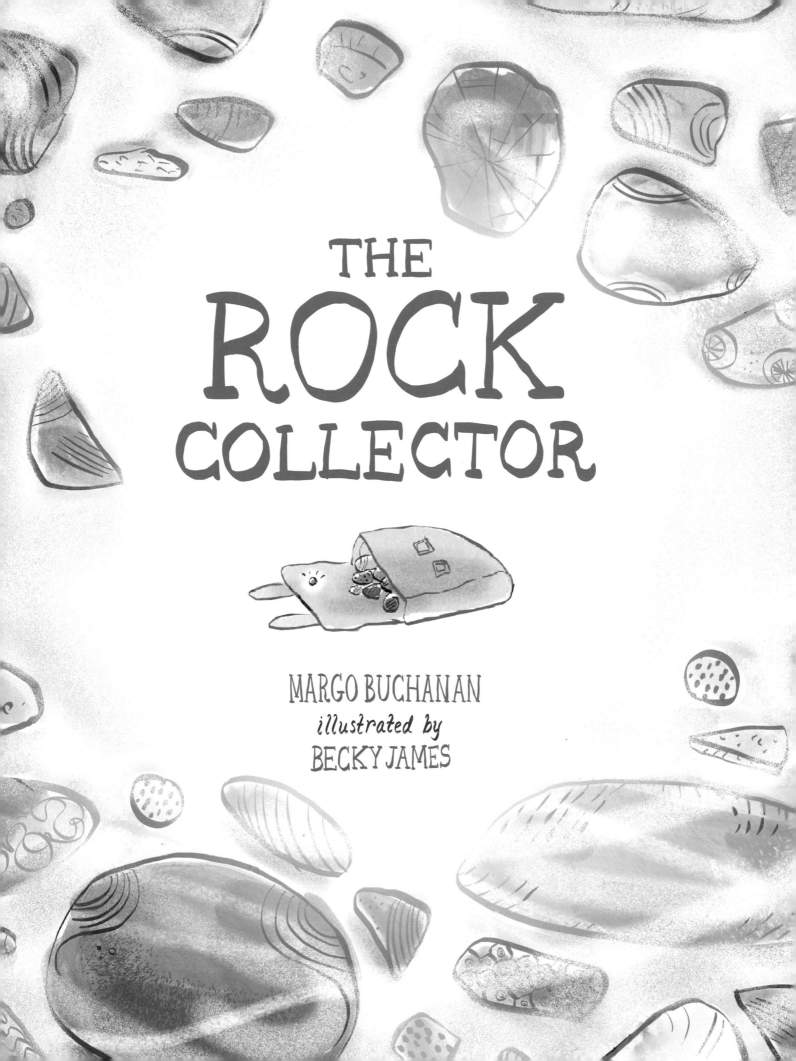

# THE
# ROCK
# COLLECTOR

MARGO BUCHANAN
*illustrated by*
BECKY JAMES

A long time ago, in a land bursting with nature...

...there lived a boy named Ashmuvara. He was taller than the other boys his age. Tall in the way that people expected more of him.

His arrow was so quick, so precise, that his village nicknamed him...

*Ash The Flash!*

His strength
and speed were admired by
countless villagers for miles around.

When the world looked at Ashmuvara, they saw a champion. An archery legend.

THE VILLAGE GAZETTE

ASH WINS AGAIN!

THIS KID IS UNSTOPPABLE!

"THAT'S MY BOY!!"

From a young age, he had never lost a competition, never missed a shot.

But nine-year-old Ashmuvara didn't really care for archery or competing. He was a gentle and thoughtful boy, captivated by the beauty of nature.

He wanted to know how the world came to be—the peaks of the mountains, the texture of the canyons, the lushness of the forest.

And rock-collecting was *his* thing.
Discovering the rocks' shapes and colors was how
he reimagined the history of the Earth. Each day, by the
riverbed, as he examined what was on offer, he felt *alive*.

One Sunday morning, when the sky was blue and there was a light breeze swirling through the trees, Ashmuvara set out with Papa for the amphitheater for the archery finals. It was Ashmuvara's last competition of the season. And like every other competition that had come before it, he was poised to win.

Because they had set off early—as parents *always* seem to insist—
Papa let Ashmuvara take the footpath to the riverbed at the edge of
the forest, while he carried on directly through thc main road.

"Don't be late! We have a match to win, boy!" shouted Papa,
raising a clenched fist in anticipated victory.

But Ashmuvara didn't hear him. Once he was in the forest, the world was quiet and still. So quiet that he could hear the soft chorus of frogs tickling his ears while the smell of evergreen filled his lungs. As he approached the riverbed, he felt his toes jingle and his fingers jangle, and for a second he thought he could hear his heart sing...

"The world is abundant, generous and free— so many amazing rocks just waiting for me!"

Ashmuvara walked through the wet mud, picking up rocks, putting some in his rucksack...

...setting others down, losing track of time...

Until he came upon Ganesha, munching on
a tower of lotus cakes.

"Hey Ganesha!" Ashmuvara jumped with surprise.
"I didn't see you there!"

"You'd be surprised how often that happens." Ganesha
smiled, continuing his feast. "Don't you have a
competition today?"

"I do." Ashmuvara sighed.

"Ah what's the matter, boy? Aren't you expected to win?"

"It's just that"—paused Ashmuvara, flatly
—"winning, winning, winning, all this village cares
about is winning! I sometimes wonder if they even like archery."

"*Uh hmm...*" Ganesha pondered. "About the winning, is it?" he
asked while rubbing his necklace of 108 mala beads.

# Tooo Tooo Tooo Toooo!

The loud sound of a trumpet coming from the
amphitheater interrupted Ganesha's musing.
Ashmuvara scrambled to his feet.
The competition had started.

## He was late!

THUMP
THUMP
THUMP...

CRUNCH CRUNCH CRUNCH...

Ashmuvara's feet hit the leaves as he ran through the forest at full speed. In the clearing, up ahead, was Papa, waving his arms frantically, when suddenly...

# SPLAT!

Ashmuvara tripped and fell face first on his hands, skimming his cheek and twisting his ankle.

He lay sprawled on the ground, dazed. Before he could open his mouth to say *ouch*, Papa raced over, jerked him to his feet, and said, "You're okay, boy!"

Ashmuvara's mouth fell open in protest. Everything in his body told him that wasn't true: his ankle throbbing with pain, his eyes swelling with tears. He sucked in a breath and hoped that if he didn't let his tears fall that maybe the pain would go away.

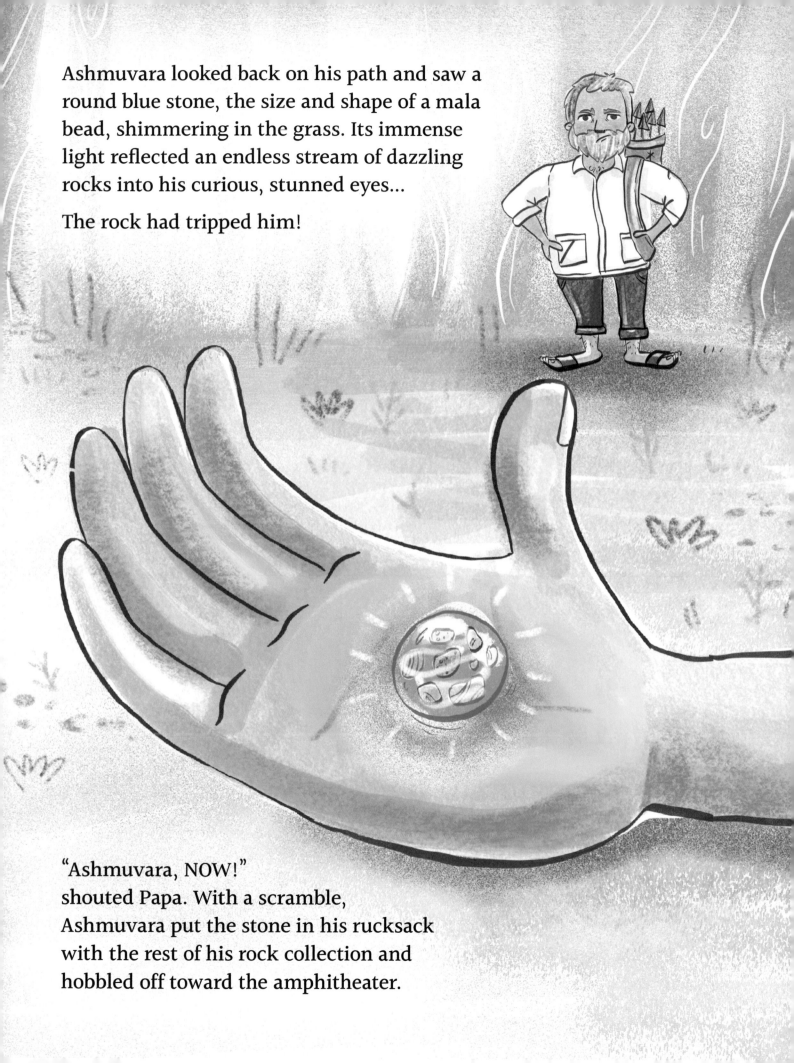

Ashmuvara looked back on his path and saw a round blue stone, the size and shape of a mala bead, shimmering in the grass. Its immense light reflected an endless stream of dazzling rocks into his curious, stunned eyes...

The rock had tripped him!

"Ashmuvara, NOW!"
shouted Papa. With a scramble,
Ashmuvara put the stone in his rucksack
with the rest of his rock collection and
hobbled off toward the amphitheater.

As he walked, something curious started to happen...

His bag got **heavier**...

...and **heavier**...

...and *even* heavier...!

Ashmuvara arrived. *Barely*.

He lined up to join his competitors who were ready with their bows drawn. Papa was cheering. Papa's friends were cheering. The whole village was so rowdy with excitement that their shouting *Ash the Flash! Ash the Flash!* made the ground tremble.

The bell rang and the arrows started to fly toward their target. The throbbing pain in Ashmuvara's ankle was so distracting that, with each attempt, his arrow missed the bull's eye.

Ashmuvara stood there, baffled by his first loss *ever*. His heart sunk when he glanced at Papa in the crowd, whose face was buried in his hands.

Ashmuvara left immediately, avoiding the gazes of the people he had let down and hampered by the weight of his rucksack, whose heaviness—inexplicably—continued to grow...

This time, eager to escape the day, he took the shortest way home.

When he arrived, he caught sight of Pree, his big sister (though only half his height), sobbing into her hands through the side window.

Ashmuvara had always wanted to be *just like her*. He worshipped her, as younger brothers quietly do. He knew he often annoyed her, but he also knew she loved him fiercely, too.

Ashmuvara dragged his rock collection onto the coffee table and tenderly put an arm over his big sister. "What is it, Pree?" he asked.

"It's Freya." Pree sobbed. "She said that"—Pree paused to catch her breath—"she is best friends with Maia now... I feel so, so, so..." She trailed off, unable to say anything more.

"Pree?" Ashmuvara said nervously, unsure of himself. "I–I–I never really liked Freya, you know. Ugh, I mean"—he fumbled—"you know she can be really bossy sometimes." Ashmuvara hoped something he said would make Pree peer out from behind her hands, which were now spilling with tears.

"Actually, come to think of it, Maia can be bossy, too!" Ashmuvara carried on, though he could see that nothing was working.

He finally took a big sigh. This was another defeat in his awful day.

Exhausted, Ashmuvara let his head fall onto his big sister's shoulder. He looked in bewilderment at the shiny blue rock shimmering on the table in front of him. He picked it up. Disappointing Papa hurt more than the sting of losing.

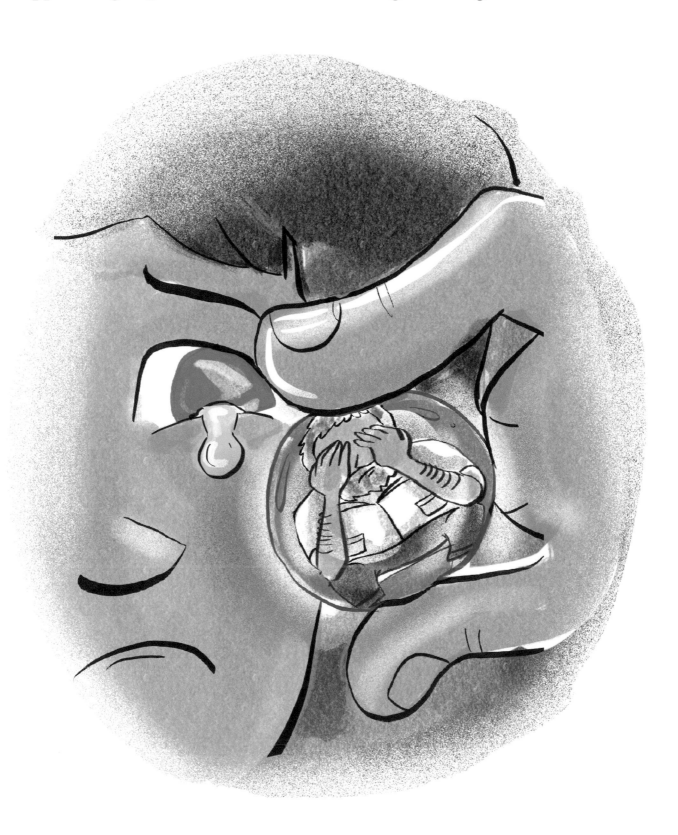

Ashmuvara also didn't know what his sister needed to hear to feel better. So he decided to stop guessing and, with a deep belly breath, he said the truest thing that was in his heart, "Pree"—he sighed— "I feel sad, too."

Pree squeezed her brother hard around his waist. He surrendered to the downpour of tears he had fought so hard to keep back all afternoon. Cuddled up on the couch with his sister, Ashmuvara realized how good it felt to finally cry.

Evening arrived. As the siblings drifted off to sleep, Papa came home and tiptoed in. And the village was, well, *mostly* still.

The next morning, Ashmuvara awoke to find that the throbbing in his ankle had waned.

Papa came in from the kitchen with tea and bread and sat next to him to help him gather his rocks back into his rucksack, when Ashmuvara noticed that one was missing.

"Tough day, yesterday," said Papa.

Ashmuvara nodded, marveling at where the shiny blue rock had disappeared to.

"This morning Pree said you were the only one who made her feel better yesterday," continued Papa.

"Yeah," Ashmuvara replied. "When I gazed into the rock that tripped me I could see how much sadness I was carrying around...and Prcc too!"

Papa smiled gently. "Why don't you skip archery practice this afternoon. Let's meet at the riverbed instead," he said.

Ashmuvara beamed back at Papa. He stood up, and as he threw his rucksack behind his shoulder, he realized its heaviness was gone! It was as light as it had been yesterday morning before his encounter with the shiny blue rock.

"Okay, Papa." Ashmuvara smiled.

"Excellent!" Papa grinned back at him with the confidence of a man who had seen his son for the very first time. "I'll meet you there, my boy."

As Ashmuvara skipped out the door, he felt a wave of gratitude wash over him. It was a funny feeling—to be thankful for the obstacles sent his way yesterday. Ashmuvara's chest expanded with a sense of possibility, and the mountains and the forest and the animals all joined his heart singing:

"The world is abundant, generous, and free—
all the twists and turns are happening *for me!*"